For a long time I would go to bed, happy, with my books and a flashlight. As soon as I'd turn it on, characters would come flooding out of the pages. Flocks of them. Neighbors, horses, birds, ambidextrous Martians, timid heroes, evildoers, supermen and superwomen, traitors, harmless or enchanted characters, the falsely accused, the invisible, the tunnel-dwelling, along with cherubs and imprisoned princesses. No one will ever know how many of us gathered there, underneath the covers.

This book is dedicated to all those characters, and to their creators who invented the world of children's books and who, day after day, continue to nurture ideas for new stories. For the endless days and nights of reading, I thank them from the bottom of my heart and my warm bed.

Claude Ponti

For my parents
C.P.

Claude Ponti

Translated from the French by
Alyson Waters and Margot Kerlidou

It's ding ding tweet tweet o'clock in the morning!
Blaze, the masked chicklet, is responsible for waking up all the other chicklets.
There are ten days left until Bertha Daye's party. Not a day, not a minute more.

Today is Day 1. After today, there will only be 9 days left.
Every morning without fail, the chicklets wake up and leap out of their beds. They try to jump as far as they can.

The chicklets are Bertha Daye's best friends, and Bertha Daye is their best friend, too.
For the party, they want to build her the most unbelievalicious castle of all cakes. And . . . it will be a surprise.

Bertha's other best friends live here and there and everywhere and sometimes very far away. Luckily, the Mailybirds know everyone's address. On the afternoon of Day 1, the chicklets make invitations for all of Bertha Daye's other best friends. Blaze writes a simple guide for the chicklets to follow:

"Come one, come all! This Sunday we'll be having a surprise celebration for Bertha Daye. There will be
an irrisistablicious castle cake. Signed, the chicklets." But the chicklets just write whatever they feel like.
So while Plaige copies from Rizm, Kan and Dinsky start sticking on the stamps.

On the morning of Day 2, the chicklets set off to Olga Layitall's to gather some eggs.
Blaze shows the others how to choose the right kind of egg.
They must only gather castle eggs – certainly never chicklet eggs . . .

. . . and never ever snowman or car or cow eggs . . . or egg ceteras.
Otherwise, imagine what Bertha Daye's castle cake might look like! Zilch!
And nobody wants to eat zilch.

On the afternoon of Day 2, the chicklets pay a visit to the Stoutspouts.
They bathe, they nap, they divey dive, hover dive, sinky dive and skim swim,
and do other typical Stoutspout stuff.

Then they bring home the very best Stoutspouts. That way they'll have the very best water
to make the very best batter for the most incredibalicious most-bestest castle cake ever.
The chicklet with the mushroom on her head will find her way home, too. Don't worry, she always does.

On the morning of Day 3, the chicklets head off to the shores of Lake Soyummi
to get some cream from the Jumbo Cow. With the cream, they can whip up a frosting
with tasty pistachio and rosewater flavors to add to the castle cake.

Lying in the green grass, Blaze is reading a book about Blaze to see if what it says about him is true and if by any chance he might find a recipe for candied apples in it – they would make very lovely centerpieces for the party. Meanwhile, Fearless Feathergirl is flying bareback over the lake on Big Babba.

On the afternoon of Day 3, the chicklets go down into the Chocolate Mine. Deep in the mine, everything is made of chocolate: the floor, the ceiling, even the walls. The chicklets carry back as much chocolate as they can. It's simply impossible to imagine Bertha Daye's castle cake without chocolate.

It would be like a chocolate cake without chocolate, or chocolate ice cream without chocolate, or hot chocolate without chocolate. And besides, there's no such thing as chocolateless chocolate. Meanwhile, Belle Jamine Frankleen is inventing the umbrella. She'll need it on page 27.

The morning of Day 4 is for flour bagging.
Castle cake flour must be powdery soft, finer than fairy dust.

Before they can bring it home, it has to be splittersplatted. The only true way to splittersplat is to slipslide and splitside in the piles and peaks of flour. Blaze and the chicklets are doing a great job.

The afternoon of Day 4 is for sugar fetching. The chicklets walk for miles and
miles across the wooden footbridge to reach the sugar on the mountaintop.
And they take a pinch of sugar from the sea to make their foamy meringues.

With the mountaintop sugar, they'll sculpt the castle cake decorations, because mountaintop sugar is very easy to sculpt. Blaze can't find Newsflash – for once she's not reading the headlines of the day – even though he looks for her everywhere. But that's not surprising. Turns out, for a change, she's doing what everyone else is doing: fetching sugar.

The morning of Day 5 is for fruit picking all the bright, juicy, lip-smacking fruit they can find.
Fruit is the last ingredient they need.

Topsyturvy is going in the wrong direction. Snoozfesta is napping, like she always does.
Newsflash has her nose in the paper once again. Li'l Benny Goodgood is making silly faces.
As soon as the chicklets have finished picking the fruit, they'll begin blixing the batter.

On the afternoon of Day 5, they blix the batter. The chicklets work very attentively.
If the blix is botched the whole castle cake will be botched. The ingredients need to be mixed, blended, and splatulated

in the right order. For example, they've got to splatter the batter with their fat little feet and flizzatten it all the way with a rolling pin. They also have to make sure the egg whites are fine n' frothy before combining them with the sugar. And taste every cream, filling, and frosting before they can smearify them. Making a mess is an absolute necessity.

On Day 6, the chicklets build the ovens for baking the castle cake.
In the evening, they go to bed, and while they're sleeping

Blaze keeps an eye on the ovens. All night. On Day 7, Blaze and the chicklets do nothing at all.
They rest. So peacefully you can't even see them.

On the morning of Day 8, Blaze, the masked chicklet, wakes up all the other chicklets.
It's ding ding tweet tweet o'clock and there are only two days left to finish Bertha Daye's castle cake.

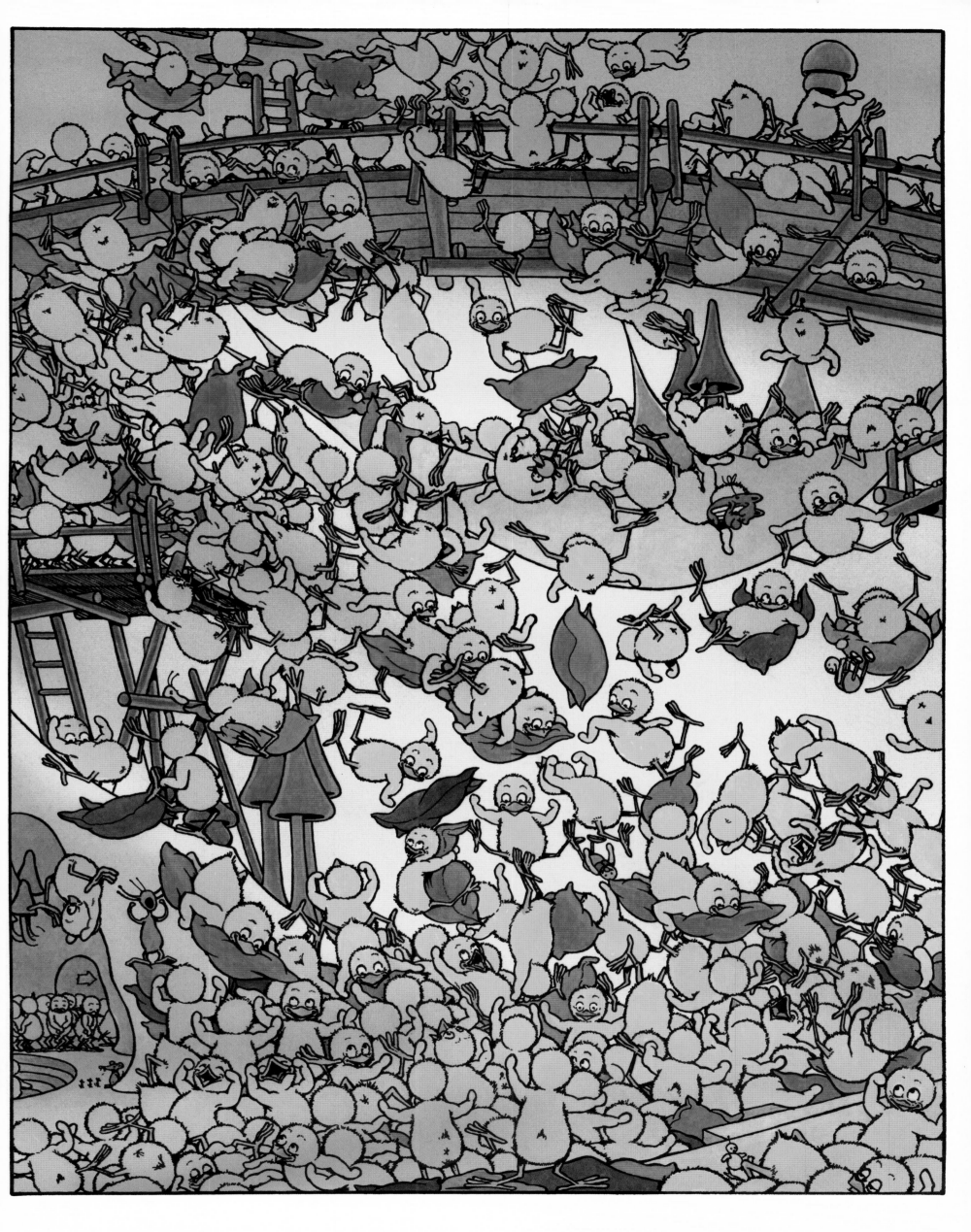

Not a day or a minute more until the party. All the guests will be there and everything has to be ready. Everything. But with the chicklets, there's nothing to fear. Everything they do, they do well.

On the afternoon of Day 8, Blaze is heading up the teams responsible for the castle cake's finishing touches.
All the layers of cookies and cream and chocolate and crunchy stuff and cookies and chocolate and cookies
and raspberry mousse and chocolate and cookies are now in place, one atop the other.

After they've pastry-fied the living rooms and the front door has been carved out of butter cream,
all the chicklets decorate the castle cake, inside and out. All of them, that is, except for Cirkiss-Perkiss,
who's balancing on the tip of a pole, practicing her surprise act for Bertha Daye.

On the morning of Day 9, Bertha Daye's castle cake is ready.
Not a single meringue is missing. The towers are wonderfully waffled and fluffily frosted.
Other than Hesaid and Shesaid, who are discussing important matters,

Blaze and all the other chicklets are still at home.
They're marveling at Bertha Daye's castle cake out the back window.
This moment calls for silence and wonder before the final chickcheck.

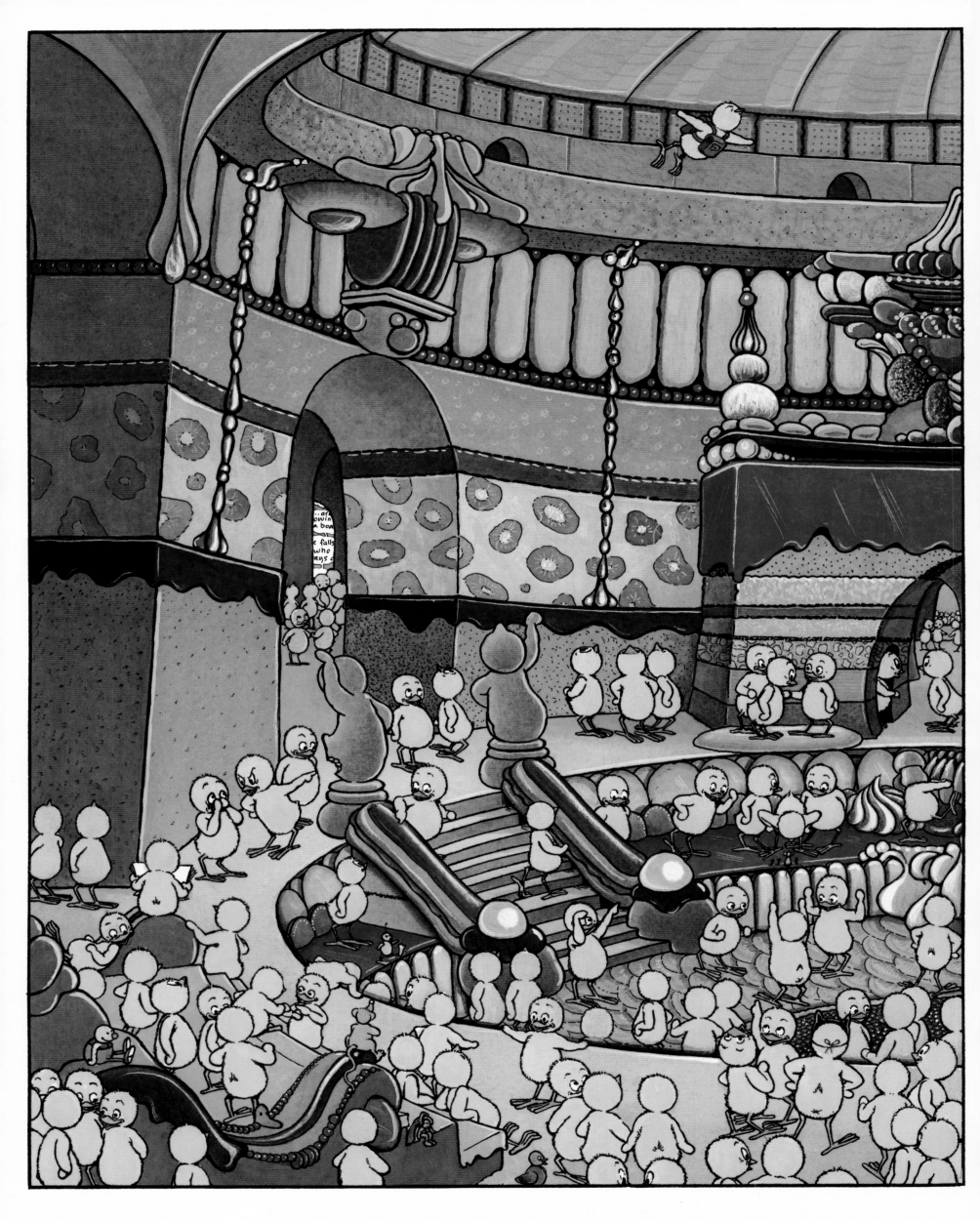

After everything's been chickchecked on Day 9, the chicklets admire their masterpiece.
They're particularly fond of the big round party room with its glossy glazes,
its éclairs, and its multi-pie floor.

The big round party room is surrounded by six medium square rooms, twelve small round or square rooms, thirty hallways made of red-berry and passion-mango sorbet, sixty soft nougat staircases, sixty butterscotch slides, two thousand three hundred and twenty-seven marshmallow pillows, and just as many made from apricots.

It's the 10th day and at 25 minutes and 67 seconds past 1 o'clock in the afternoon, the guests arrive. That's the exact time when Bertha was born.

Bertha is wearing her grown-up golden dress, her black hair in swirls, her garnet necklace, and her party smile. She is delighted. She has so many friends, and just as many presents!

It's a celebration. Inside the castle cake everybody feasts on castle cake.
Bertha Daye is no exception.

There's just so much of it, and it's so irresistiblisciously incredibliscious,
that the festivities last days and days and no one knows how many.

Tomorrow, however, when the last crumb of the last bite of castle cake
has been eaten, everybody will go back home.

But no matter where they all may go, no matter how many castle cakes they may taste,
everyone will agree that Bertha Daye's was the best in the whole wide world. Because it's true.

And then, at the very end of the next day, night falls. And like every other night every other time, the chicklets all take up their places and positions for bedtime. Every single chicklet except one . . .

Text and illustrations copyright © Claude Ponti, 2004
English-language translation copyright © Alyson Waters and Margot Kerlidou, 2021
Originally published by L'école des loisirs as *Blaise et le château d'Anne Hiversère*, 2004, Paris
First English-language edition, Elsewhere Editions, 2022

Library of Congress Cataloging-in-Publication Data available upon request.

Elsewhere Editions, 232 3rd Street #A111, Brooklyn, New York
www.elsewhereeditions.org

Distributed by Penguin Random House
www.penguinrandomhouse.com

This work was made possible by the New York State Council on the Arts with the support
of Governor Andrew M. Cuomo and the New York State Legislature. Funding for the
translation of this book was provided by a grant from the Carl Lesnor Family Foundation.
This publication was made possible with support from Lannan Foundation, the National
Endowment for the Arts, Cornelia and Michael Bessie Foundation,
and the New York City Department of Cultural Affairs.

PRINTED IN CHINA